FIND OUT MOONSHINE

FIND OUT MOONSHINE

PETER A. HEASLEY

On the cover:

August Malmström: *Dancing Fairies* (1866). Nationalmuseum (Photo: Nationalmuseum), public domain. Flipped horizontally by the author.

ISBN 979-8-9911606-2-9 (paperback)
ISBN 979-8-9911606-3-6 (ebook)

peteraheasley.com

For those who can't remember

1

From their perch in the darkness, ten thousand cicadas sang a chorus for a hot Texas night. Sitting on his porch, John "Boogie" Bouguereau practiced actor's diction with the help of a YouTube video. The lights of the truck belonging to his friend, Lottie, began breaking through the trees lining the road, a vision of gold through the shadows. When Lottie parked in the short stretch of dirt that served for a driveway, those same headlights bleached all the color from the world. Boogie kept articulating his T's. Lottie flashed his high beams. Boogie gave Lottie the finger. Lottie honked. Boogie stood and put his phone in his pocket. He walked through a cloud of gnats that had gathered in front of Lottie's headlights and opened the passenger-side door.

"Hey, Boogie. How you been?" Lottie said.

Boogie sat in the passenger seat. "Good, man. Just working on my high score there. Glad to see you freed up for once."

"Carly's out at her folks' place this weekend with the kids. Her dad's not doing too well."

"That's too bad," Boogie said. "So, what're you thinking?"

"We could go to Scully's, hit our old stompin' grounds."

"With all them rednecks?"

"You're a redneck, Boogie. You live in a double-wide and spend all your free time fishing."

"I just call that being a free man."

"Well, let me tell you. I got a girlfriend and two kids. I don't get too much 'free man' time."

"Well, hell, then. Let's go to Scully's and pick a fight or something."

"That's the spirit."

Lottie drove them down dark country roads. With a new moon hidden away on the other side of the Earth, a broken sheet of clouds closed off the universe to all but a few of the brightest stars. Boogie couldn't find much to say. That would change before a live audience at Scully's.

Lottie broke Boogie's meditation to say, "What's that light on ahead? Something new?"

"I don't usually take Route 6. Let's go check it out."

Once in the parking lot, the truck hummed while Boogie leaned over the dashboard to ponder the building, a glass and metal mushroom decked in neon.

"Build-A-Burger," Lottie said. "Who knows, this could be better than eating at Scully's. Nora's nachos always give me heartburn."

"Looks like we're the only ones here, though," Boogie said.

"Because we're in the middle of nowhere," Lottie said. "Musta just opened. There's a girl inside."

Boogie ran his hands through his hair. "I don't have a good feeling."

Lottie walked out of the truck and into the restaurant.

"Alright, then," Boogie said.

The parking lot was empty, and grass grew in the cracks. Boogie caught the front door as it closed behind Lottie. Inside, the restaurant was clean and bright and smelled more like cleaning spray than grilled meat. As Boogie reached the counter, Lottie turned around. He shook his head slightly. Boogie looked past him, to the girl behind the counter. Despite his own uncertain feeling before, Boogie, always the actor, would take Lottie's uncertainty as a challenge.

"Good evening," Boogie said to the cashier. "How are you this fine summer evening?"

"I am fine, thank you," she said, like a metronome.

"How long you been open?" Boogie asked.

"May I take your order?" she said.

Boogie looked at Lottie, who shrugged.

Lottie turned to the cashier. "Uh, yeah, let's see here." He stroked his chin. "Let's build it, then. Double cheeseburger, bacon, barbecue sauce. When the cat's away, as they say."

With a straight index finger, the girl pressed several buttons on the register. "I will be right back. Just one moment." She went around to the kitchen.

"You see or hear anyone else working here?" Lottie said.

Boogie looked around. The restaurant was furnished in a retro style, with bright red vinyl booths, chrome stools at the window bar, and a silent jukebox. The stools did not all match each other, though, and the red booths were too close together. Above the hanging lights, some multicolored LEDs ran along an otherwise black ceiling. When Boogie blocked the lights with his hand to better see the ceiling, they grew brighter. Blinding white light dissolved all but the darkest shadows in the restaurant, and Boogie closed his eyes.

A few seconds later, when it seemed like the lights had dimmed again, Boogie reopened his eyes. He could see nothing but a uniform gray color all around and could not find where the walls met the floor or the ceiling. Lottie was standing next to him, in full color.

"What just happened?" Lottie said. "Am I blind? I don't see nothing but you, Boogie."

"Me, too," Boogie said. "I knew something was wrong, I knew it. Could feel it in my gut before we got here. Damn it all to hell."

"Alright, alright. Let's see. Two options, far as I can see. One," Lottie said, then he turned around. His body jerked.

Boogie turned around, too.

Three gray aliens stood before him and Lottie, each about four feet tall and each with a taut face built around two large black eyes and a small menacing mouth.

Boogie had the vague sensation of falling, as if his knees had given way, and his muscles twitched to keep him erect. "Why is it always the rednecks?" he said flatly. "They always take the rednecks."

Lottie looked at him, wide-eyed, nostrils flaring.

"'Cause no one'll believe us is why," Boogie said, answering his own question. "Alright. Let's stay calm and see what they want. There's a way through this. There's always a way through."

The three aliens stood silently, staring at the two men.

"They want us to speak?" Lottie said. His hands were shaking.

"I don't know," Boogie replied, not taking his eyes off them.

"I thought they'd speak telepathically or something."

"Maybe they're trying, but we got no brains."

"Man, this ain't no time for jokes," Lottie said.

Boogie, with a loud and clear voice, said, "Hello. My name is Boogie. John Bouguereau. This is Lottie, that is, Lancelot Meadrow the Third."

The three aliens did not respond.

"What now, Boogie?" Lottie said.

Boogie held out his hand.

"Careful, man," Lottie said quietly.

"Just, maybe they'll respond to politeness."

Slowly, the alien in front of Boogie stepped forward and reached out its hand, a bundle of wrinkled gray fingers like a chicken's foot. As Boogie wrapped his fingers around the alien's cold, dead-fish grip, the room filled with black.

Boogie found himself in another room and saw Lottie standing there. The room was oddly shaped, its four walls meeting at unusual angles. The longest wall, to his right, was semicircular, or almost so, covered in fake wood paneling from the 1970s and somewhat shabbily put together. A red-shaded lamp hung low from the metal ceiling, over a six-sided card table wrapped in green felt. Seated at the table, on wooden stools, were four gray aliens, each wearing a hat of cheap, theme-park quality. From one of the hats dangled a price tag. Above them, on the wood-paneled wall, a painting of dogs playing poker hung crookedly.

Lottie and Boogie looked at each other.

"What now, man?" Lottie said.

"Good evening," Boogie said to the seated aliens.

They did not raise their heads or respond.

After a long, anxious minute, another gray alien walked in from behind the two men. It stretched out one arm as if inviting Lottie and Boogie to take a seat at the table with the other four.

Lottie and Boogie looked at each other and at the table, wide-eyed and uncertain.

"Okay," Boogie said. "Maybe they just want to play cards or something, you know, establish amicable relations."

"Could be," Lottie said, shuffling forward on the smooth obsidian floor. "Look, check your stool for probes and things before sitting down."

Boogie did as his friend suggested and felt only chewed gum under his stool. He sat across from Lottie at the card table, with two aliens seated between them on each side.

Boogie looked past an alien wearing a sombrero toward the one who had invited them to sit down. It was standing at the corner of the far wall, but it did not meet his gaze. The aliens seated with him were holding playing cards in their hands. Boogie picked up the cards in front of him. Lottie copied his friend and said, with a shaking voice, "So, what's the game? Draw, stud, hold 'em?"

With slow, deliberate movements, the four aliens folded up their cards and passed them forward to Lottie, their gestures synchronized like robots on an assembly line.

Lottie took the cards. He felt them and rubbed them against each other. "These could have come off any store shelf," he said.

Boogie could smell the wood paneling, and the table

itself gave off a sort of musty odor, as if the aliens had pulled it out of someone's basement.

Lottie went through the deck and pulled out the two jokers, putting them in his shirt pocket. "Okay, maybe draw is easiest to start with," he said.

Boogie gently nodded.

Lottie shuffled nervously, dropping a few cards onto the table. He laughed at himself.

The aliens did not respond in any way.

Lottie dealt himself, Boogie, and the four aliens five cards each, flicking the cards away from his body with some regained skill Boogie was glad to see.

The aliens picked up the cards very slowly, demonstrating, as they did, some deficit of digital dexterity.

"Here," Boogie said, laying his cards out on the table and nodding at Lottie. "For starters, let's just lay our cards down, and we'll all learn together. We'll go from there. How's that sound?"

The aliens, without turning their heads, kept struggling to pick up their cards.

Lottie laid his own cards down, and, half a minute later, the aliens followed suit.

"Alright," Boogie said. "They recognize you as the dealer. They'll do what you do."

Lottie sighed. "You think they understand us at all?"

Boogie shrugged.

Lottie looked toward the alien in the sombrero then at the cards in front of it. "Okay, you've got two pair, threes and sevens. Not bad." Casting his eyes upward again, he searched for some kind of response but found none. "Let's get you one card." He flipped up from the pile. "Four. Boogie? Your turn."

Boogie spread out the cards of an alien wearing a pink plastic fedora and helped it to a near straight. He then took care of his own hand and came up with a flush. An alien in a felt Alpine hat came up with a pair of aces.

Lottie then helped the alien wearing a newsboy cap much too small for his bulbous head and said to him, "You, sir, I'm afraid, have nothin'. Alright, I've got two fours, and the rest is garbage, but I like this king in my hand, so I'm going to draw two." He did and got another king with a seven. "Hot dog," he said. "But Boogie wins with a flush."

Boogie looked up at the alien standing in the corner, who gazed back but made no response.

"I guess we keep going. Your turn to deal, my friend," Lottie said to the alien in the sombrero.

The little gray alien took the cards that Lottie and Boogie had collected and stacked for it. It proceeded to shuffle but fumbled with the cards, going very slowly.

It went so slowly that Boogie, watching it, began to lose focus. To fill the time, he looked around at everything in the room, at the paneled wall and shining black floor. The wall across from the wood-paneled wall was shorter, straight, and made of some kind of white, translucent glass on which various signs and symbols began to appear, all in black. "Hey, Lottie," he whispered, motioning to the wall with his chin.

Lottie looked over, and, as he focused on it, the black lines and symbols faded away.

The sombrero alien continued to deal the hand with

the urgency and deftness of an earthworm and would have dealt each six cards had Boogie not stopped it, holding both palms up to the alien. Once again, they all laid their cards up, and Lottie and Boogie showed their neighbors how to make a hand.

Lottie declared the newsboy-cap alien the winner, with a full house. No enthusiasm or response of any kind showed on its face. Lottie smiled and was very close to patting the alien on the back but stopped suddenly when a wave of terrifying heat washed through the room.

At that moment, the alien who had been their guide gestured the two men toward a traditional-looking wooden door on the wall behind Boogie, presumably the door through which they had come, or would have come, had they not somehow teleported into this room.

As the men got up from their stools, Lottie brushed his hands across the back of his jeans, checking for holes.

"Gentlemen, it's been a pleasure," Boogie said and bowed a little.

Both men had to stoop their heads and shoulders to pass through the door and into a space beyond, which was dark except for one strong overhead light. Standing up straight again, Boogie heard the door click behind them. A breeze passed by.

"We're back in the parking lot," Lottie said. "Look. There's nothing here. No Build-A-Burger."

"What?" Boogie asked. "Why would there be a Build-A-Burger here? We're in the middle of nowhere."

Lottie pulled his head back and looked around. "Right....

Why are we out here anyway? What did you wanna show me?"

"Me? Beats me. You're the one driving."

"Alright. Whatever. Let's get on to Scully's, then. The wolf's howling for some nachos."

Half an hour later, Boogie caught himself staring blankly over an empty tray of nachos. He stretched his arms and looked around the bar.

"Same old crowd," Lottie said.

"Yep," Boogie said.

"You looking around for something else, then? You'd know if she was here."

"What? No. Just...."

"Come on, man. Let that fish swim away already. It's been eight years since high school," Lottie said.

"I was just looking to see who's here, that's all. Maybe there're some other little fishies who need me to cast my rod in their direction, reel 'em in, you know?"

Lottie laughed. "Hey, what's this?" He pulled two joker cards out of his shirt pocket. "Now, how in the hell did these get in here?"

"Whatcha got there?"

"Two jokers. One for each of us. That's us, Boogie. Two jokers. Kids prolly put 'em in there. Here. Take yours, joker man."

The two drank. No more than two words left their lungs at any one time.

Lottie yawned and pinched his eyes. "Is it just me, or does it feel a bit later than it is?"

"That's just you catching up now, with the girls away."

"Must be."

At that, someone made a boisterous entrance into the loud bar. Boogie strained not to turn.

"Don't even turn around, Boogie. It's not worth it. Just drink your beer in peace."

Boogie nodded and drank while Andie announced her presence to anyone who would listen. He gripped the handle of his heavy pint glass tightly and pressed it against the table.

Lottie saw this and said, "You know what? It's not such a bad night outside. Why don't we drive around a bit, have a few beers at my place?"

"Sorry I'm not my usual entertaining self," Boogie said.

"A little Call of Duty will fix that. When the cat's away, as they say."

At those words, a pattern flashed in Boogie's mind, like cursive writing on a bright computer tablet, then it disappeared. He left some cash on the table and followed Lottie out to the truck.

2

"Whoa there, Andie," Boogie said, as she stumbled into the side of his truck. "Hey, whatcha thinking? Maybe that's enough for one night."

It was a week after his night out with Lottie.

Andie looked up at the crescent moon. From this angle, her turned-down mouth looked to Boogie like everything the shining moon was not, a satellite of sadness.

"Find out moonshine, Andie."

"What?"

"Find out moonshine."

Andie narrowed her eyes at Boogie. She went for another swig of beer, but the bottle was empty.

"I'm jus' gonna have to...kiss the moon!"

"That's it, go on, kiss the moon goodnight."

"I can't reach."

"Well, blow it a kiss, then."

And she did.

"Come on. I'll take you home."

"You wish, mister boogey man," Andie said, holding the door handle for balance.

"Alright, then. Take a cab or wait for one of these rednecks to make you a better offer," Boogie said as he got into the truck.

Andie slid into the truck with more coordination than Boogie expected.

"You still down on Livingston Lane?" Boogie said, though he knew exactly where she lived.

"Mmm...hm," she said, stroking the dashboard with her two index fingers.

"Alright, then." He pulled out of the Scully's parking lot.

Andie looked out of the side window, silently.

Boogie enjoyed the silence, for it meant she was no longer putting on a show. He felt a bit like her rescuer; he wanted her to sit silently with him all the time. He savored the minutes they spent while the moon smiled crookedly above them.

"Hey, this is it, right?" Boogie said.

"Yessir," she said, looking at the small dark house she had grown up in.

"Well, maybe you better get yourself in there. Get some rest."

"Yes, Daddy," she said, putting on her act again.

"That's it—git to bed before I whoop ya." He smiled.

She kissed the three long fingers of her hand and smushed them into his right cheek.

"Get on in there," he said warmly.

She walked up to the front door, stumbling once, and fumbled for her keys for a while. He looked at her in her loose blouse and tight jeans. She opened the front door and went in without turning back to him.

He waited for her to close the front door, but she did not.

Boogie sat there, engine running, headlights on her garage door, looking at the glowing red gauges on the dashboard. He looked up again at her open door. His hands gripped the wheel. The six-cylinder sent its idling promise through his bones and blood. Sadness welled into his lower lip.

Lottie called.

The two men drove in Boogie's truck from Lottie's house toward a lake, where some cousin of a friend or a friend of a cousin was having a party that promised fireworks.

"Carly don't mind you being out like this?" Boogie asked.

The crescent moon still smiled menacingly.

"Mind? Hell, it's her cousin's place. All the better to keep an eye on me."

"And her dad?"

"Taking a turn for the worse."

Boogie stopped the truck before a train signal and waited, engine idling. He looked both ways down the tracks and saw nothing. "Now, where is this train?"

At those words, a brilliant white light shined all around them.

Boogie found himself standing with Lottie in a small room that was oddly shaped and poorly decorated according to someone's idea of Japanese style. Rice-paper screens leaned against the longest wall in the room, forming a slight curve. At each end of this wall, two other walls angled inward toward a short wall made of white glass. In front of the rice-paper screens lay a massage bed.

"Boogie?" Lottie asked tersely.

"Yes, Lottie?"

"Where are we?"

"I do not know, sir."

"Did I miss something, or did we go from the railroad tracks to this, uh, environment?"

"That is my recollection."

Boogie heard a door open behind him. A young woman in an ill-fitting kimono walked stiffly past the two men and to the bed, where she nodded, extended her hand, and smiled awkwardly. Boogie struggled to place her. Just then, a gray alien, about four feet tall, slid past him and stood next to her.

"Oh!" Boogie jumped. "Oh," he said again calmly. "You remember this, Lottie. This is the girl from the Build-A-Burger that had no burgers."

"Yes, yes, I do remember now. We played poker with these fellas."

The little gray alien extended its impossibly thin arm toward the bed, its serpentine fingers subtly flexing as it did.

"Well, what now?" Lottie said. "The poker thing didn't go so bad before. Maybe we're just doing them a small favor, you know, science. You...wanna try?"

"You asking me to go first?"

Lottie looked at him and shrugged. "You know, wife and kids and all."

"She ain't your wife."

"Well, same thing."

"If you say so," Boogie said, and he stepped forward to the table. He began to unbutton his shirt. "But ask Carly if she feels the same way about it."

"Just your shoes and socks, sir," the woman uttered, each syllable distinct.

"Al-right...." Boogie sat on the side of the bed and removed his boots and socks. He glanced at the alien, who registered no response but walked toward another door, presumably leading to the next room, and stood there as if guarding it.

"Now, please lie down on your back," the woman said.

Boogie lay on his back. The woman walked toward his feet, and when she touched them, he stiffened then relaxed.

"She feel weird?" Lottie asked.

"No, no, not really. Just...I mean, the situation's a bit weird."

"You think?"

"Hey. Take a picture. We didn't think of that last time."

"Good thinking." Lottie reached for his phone but could not find it. "I left my phone in your truck."

"Take mine, then." Boogie fished his phone out of the lower right pocket of his cargo pants and handed it to Lottie.

The phone flashed with each shot, briefly bleaching the natural colors of the scene with a sickly hue that captured more accurately the strange situation.

"Everything coming out?" Boogie said.

"Looks like it." He turned toward the alien and raised the phone in a gesture of asking permission. It made no response, so he took a few shots. "The wall is doing its squiggly line thing again."

"It's recording our thoughts and feelings or something," Boogie said.

The woman was not massaging his feet so much as

pressing her thumbs into them at various points, like a surveyor's rod on the rolling land.

"What's that above your head, on the ceiling there?" Lottie asked.

Boogie looked at the image taped to the metal ceiling. "It's that old drawing, you know, of the ideal man, by Leonardo da Vinci."

"You would know something like that."

"Well, someone's got to. Besides, it keeps me from having to look at the girl."

Lottie looked at the girl, who was staring blankly in the direction of Boogie's face. "What, you don't like the girl?"

Boogie turned his face toward Lottie and knit his brow a little.

Lottie came around near Boogie's head and looked at her. "I guess I don't see the problem so much," he said. "Just a blank gaze."

"I maybe don't want to say with her hands vised across my feet, but she's sort of gone, you know? Like, alive, but soulless. Those big black eyes are empty. Evil, or something. Can you hear me, young lady?"

She did not answer.

"I rest my case," Boogie said. "She ain't all there."

"Can't be worse than old bug eyes here," Lottie muttered. "How long is she going to do that?"

"Beats me, man."

With that, the woman stopped, stood erect, and let her arms hang stiffly at her side. "There you go. All better."

Boogie quickly sprang up, hopped off the table, grabbed his shoes and socks, and sat on the floor to put them back on. The woman, meanwhile, was gesturing to Lottie to lie down. Boogie watched as he took off his shoes and socks and lay down, staring first at the woman then at the Vitruvian Man.

Boogie took the phone from Lottie's hand.

Lottie said, "No pictures of me. I could explain till I turned blue in the face that I was abducted by aliens, but all Carly would see is that I went to some massage parlor to get jerked off."

Boogie sat against the angled wall of the room. "You think we're in space right now? We could be, like, light-years away."

"Maybe, but last time they dropped us off right where we started. No, this is some alternative dimension or something. That's why we didn't remember it last time."

"But we had those cards as a souvenir. Now we've got some pictures, little Dorian Gray included."

"You named him Dorian?"

"It's a literary reference. Never mind."

"You and your hobbies, man."

Boogie sat silently, staring at the gray alien. "Excuse me, sir," he said, but the creature made no response. "May we ask some questions about our situation? This seems like a good moment to make acquaintances."

The alien stared at nothing in particular and did not flinch.

Boogie looked at the wall, on which lines, squiggles, and symbols disappeared as quickly as they appeared. He looked at Lottie, who seemed to be studying the woman's face. "You think they're just, like, scientists or something? Biologists from Alpha Centauri?" Boogie asked.

"You got me. But I will say that this feels less like a massage and more like she's studying, you know, feeling. All the nerves end in the feet. You get pretty sensitive to that in a house full of Legos."

"I wouldn't mind a house full of Legos."

"Well, just put yourself out there. Step one is letting go of Andie."

"You know, Lottie, I'm looking pretty hard here, and from this angle and all the other angles we've had, I've concluded that this species of entity before me is without genitalia."

Lottie chuckled and turned his head but could not see. He chuckled again. He began laughing uncontrollably, snorting and huffing.

"You all right, there?" Boogie asked.

Lottie, wiping tears from his eyes, said, "Where the hell are we, man? What the hell are we doing? Look at us, getting massages from alien girls, her pimp looking on."

Boogie felt a flash of hot anger fill the room.

The woman stopped massaging Lottie's feet and stood, shoulders drooping, arms dangling at her sides. Her jaw fell open.

Lottie breathed sharp breaths and kicked at her, but he could not reach her. He flailed on the bed.

Boogie tried to stand to help him but felt restrained against the wall. He, too, began to flail just to bring his body upward.

A bright light burst in the room, and, as his eyes adjusted, Boogie found himself on the road again, stopped at the train tracks, a long freight locomotive clanging past.

Boogie jumped in his seat.

"You alright, man?" Lottie asked. "Train scare you?"

"What? What?" Boogie huffed. "Where are we?"

"Where we've been for about five minutes, watching this train go by."

Boogie rubbed his face. "Yeah. Yeah. Just...nothing. I don't know. Got some sort of flashback or something."

"A flashback to what, exactly?"

"Nothing, I guess."

The train passed, and the gate lifted. Boogie drove the truck across the tracks and down the darkened roads.

Lottie jerked his head downward. "Where are my shoes?"

"Not on your feet?"

"No. Nor my socks."

"Did you forget to put them on when you left the house?"

"No."

"Then they're in here somewhere."

"They are not."

"O-kay.... Well, turn on the light and look."

Lottie did this, maneuvering to look behind the seat as well. He took off his seat belt and turned around.

"Whoa, there. Put your seat belt on. What if I hit a deer or something? Then your bony ass is going through my windshield. Carly will not be happy." As Lottie's face passed by Boogie's, Boogie caught a look of intense worry. "Don't worry, man. We'll find your shoes."

Lottie arrived at the party wearing flip-flop sandals

that Boogie kept in his truck for fishing. The spectacle of fireworks in the sky would keep the other partygoers from seeing Lottie's feet, Boogie had reasoned. The beers in their hands and the lively conversation wiped the worry off his old friend's face.

Boogie began taking pictures of those dancing and of those standing around, of those laughing, and of a woman crying drunkenly. When he opened the photo gallery on his phone to delete it for her, he came across a series of blurry pictures he thought he had accidentally shot with his butt or his thigh. Two or three of these pictures, though, were less blurry than the others, and showed him lying on a table, hands locked at his stomach, receiving a foot massage from some ill-defined figure he determined to be a woman. He sat down on a log near the fire, searching his memory for when he had done this or who might have taken the picture. The time stamp read two hours earlier. He found Lottie.

"You remember anything like this?" Boogie asked. "That's about the time we were on the road from your place."

Lottie studied the picture. "But you're the one with your shoes off in the picture, not me. That's clearly you on the bed because you're wearing those stupid cargo pants you have on now."

"Yeah, well, maybe you're the one who took the picture, before or after getting the same treatment yourself."

Lottie scratched his head, and his eyelids drooped. "We've got a mystery on our hands."

"Yeah. But we're in no place to figure it out right now. Maybe there was something on that train, you know, government stuff, something that messed with our minds."

"And stole my shoes?"

"And stole your shoes."

A bit later, a mostly sober Boogie drove a sodden Lottie back to his house, taking the same roads. Nothing about the drive evoked the picture—no roadside massage parlor, no other memory. He helped Lottie into the house and as far as the couch, where he collapsed. Boogie removed the flip-flops from his feet.

He came back to the truck, which was still running. The idling engine soothed his tired body. His mind could not let go of the lost moment, and he stared through the red gauges on his dashboard. He turned on his headlights, which shined on a deer in the woods beyond. Something in this glowing, white form did evoke an image in his mind, but, just as quickly, it was gone, and he drove home.

3

About a week later, under a daytime gibbous moon, Boogie and Lottie were at work, moving earth for a new suburban housing development. At the end of the work day, they walked toward the office trailer to collect their bi-weekly paychecks.

"I suppose you're no good for a night out, huh, Lottie?" Boogie asked.

"No, sorry, man. Carly's home. She wants a movie night. God only knows what kind of rom-com I've got to sit through. I suppose it's gotta be done."

"That's the tradeoff, right?"

"Well, you know. I mean, she's on the edge right now, with her dad. Just a matter of weeks or days with him. Nothing wrong with giving her a little comfort."

"Right."

Sticking their heads into the open door of the office trailer, they saw no one and called out for their supervisor, who did not respond. Boogie walked into the trailer, followed by Lottie, and they let the metal door slam behind them. This seemed to make the lights flicker.

"Hello?" Lottie called.

"Office door's closed." Boogie walked ahead and knocked. "Lou?" He turned around, squinting. "Is it brighter than normal in here?"

"I think they're on LEDs now. I've got 'em at home, too. They just look different."

Boogie turned around and knocked again. He opened the door a little and peered in. "Yo, this is weird. Come check this out, Lottie. Office is empty."

Lottie walked into the empty room behind Boogie. Four white walls of equal length and height stood between a polished black floor and a metal ceiling. "Now, what in the hell..." he said while, without really willing it, he began to close the door behind him.

"Wait a minute. Wait, Lottie, don't—" Boogie began, but Lottie had closed the door. Boogie walked over and tried to open it, but it would not budge.

"We stuck in here?" Lottie asked.

"You know where we are, right?"

"In Lou's abandoned office."

"No. We're in the alien ship."

"The alien ship. Boogie, you been drinking?" Lottie gazed at Boogie, who watched his friend's face soften with understanding. "Man...yeah. No, the room's shaped different. This one's all squared and cubed. The others were a mess."

"But these walls are not all the same. One of them is that glass wall. Look at the writing come and go."

Lottie looked at the wall running away from the door they had just closed and saw the signs and squiggles fading in and out. "Yep. Okay. Now what? There's nothing in here."

"Right. Now what?"

The two men studied the room, pressing against the walls, reaching for the ceiling, and scraping against the floor. They measured with their wingspans and determined that the room was twelve feet in every direction. Except for the writing that registered on the one wall and the flimsy trailer door to the left of it, there was nothing else to orient them.

"I guess we wait," Boogie said.

"Well, if it's gonna be like this, I'm going to take a seat."

Boogie joined Lottie on the floor. Each man sat back against opposite walls, their legs spread outward and toward each other.

"Hold on, what's this," Boogie said, unzipping his left pants pocket and pulling out a folded-up sheet of paper.

"What's with those pants?" Lottie asked.

"They're waterproof. I tuck them into my boots, and I'm dry from the waist down."

"No one else I know has gone to such great pains to find the perfect cargo pant. No wonder you ain't got a girlfriend. What's that paper, anyway?"

"One of those packing slips from Amazon."

"You couldn't throw that out with the box?"

"Not at work, you know. I don't want my personal information out there."

"What, so they can't see that you order blow-up dolls?"

"Very funny, my friend. Here, check this out," Boogie said, and he began to fold the paper. Once the airplane was complete, he tossed it toward Lottie, who fell over to grab it.

The two tossed the airplane back and forth a few times until Boogie stopped out of boredom.

"Make a loop with your arms," Lottie said. "Gotta get it through the ring."

They tossed the paper airplane back and forth for a little while longer, trying, and sometimes succeeding, to land the airplane in the loop at various angles and attitudes. Boogie let the airplane land in his lap, finally, and did not bother to pick it up again.

"Here," he said and pulled out his phone. "The pictures came out blurry last time. Maybe video is the way. Hello, this is John 'Boogie' Bouguereau, here with Lancelot 'Lottie' Meadrow, the third in a row to bear that noble name. We are currently situated on some sort of alien spacecraft, being held not so much against our will as by our own stupidity, quite possibly being tortured into boredom by little gray aliens, who are most likely watching us right now from behind this white glass screen. Say hello, Lottie."

"Hello."

Boogie turned the camera back on himself. "Dear viewer, you cannot see the aliens right now, whereas we have seen them, but in case they come on camera and terrorize us—but they haven't done that so far—you will at least believe us, in case this video becomes a lasting memorial to our legacy. Know that we two humans, of the Texan variety, have played poker with these creatures, among other things, and now await some further study for their science."

"Or their takeover," Lottie interrupted.

"Yes, or their takeover. In which case, I wish them luck in the greatly armed State of Texas. Let 'em have New York

City or Los Angeles, which are doomed to fall into the ocean anyway. Ehm...what do I say next, Lottie?"

"Maybe describe our visitors."

"Right. These are aliens of the gray variety, who may or may not be genderless. They are accompanied by a soulless hamburger witch whom they use to lure us into these uncertain situations."

"You're making it sound like we're already drunk, and it's only four p.m.," Lottie said. "Where is that girl, anyway?"

"Lancelot Meadrow, astute as ever, rightly remarks that we are now alone in this third encounter. More updates will be provided as new information becomes available. This is John 'Boogie' Bouguereau, signing out."

The two men looked around in silence.

"They look like hairless cats, don't they?" Boogie asked. "The aliens?"

Lottie breathed out a sharp laugh. "I guess so." The screen danced a little bit.

"Hey," Boogie said, "let's make the screen go crazy. Get up."

The two lumbered off the floor and stood before the white screen.

"What do we do?" Lottie asked.

"I dunno. Just do things. Here, hold this," he said, handing the phone to Lottie. He began to make gorilla gestures in front of the screen, his arms in a stiff circle swinging back and forth as he lifted each leg in turn, his lower jaw protruding. The screen saw some brief activity.

"Here, Boogie, let's show 'em our moves." The pair began to square dance, spinning each other with their arms locked. Lottie sang: "Swing your partner 'round and 'round, kick him in the balls and throw him down."

The screen registered little activity.

"I guess it don't like comedy," Boogie said.

"Alright, let's show them the depth of humanity," Lottie replied, and he recited: "To be, or not to be, that is the question." Then, holding his hands to his heart, he said, "Romeo, O Romeo, wherefore art thou, O Romeo?"

The screen reacted only a little.

"Okay, I got one," Boogie said. Looking down, he composed himself, shook his hanging arms, and began:

"If we shadows have offended,
Think of this, and all is mended.
That you have but slumbered here,
While these visions did appear.
And this weak and idle theme,
No more yielding than a dream... uh...
Now to 'scape the serpent's tongue,
We will make amends here long;
Give me your hands, if we be friends,
And Boogie shall restore amends."

"That's, uh, wow, Boogie. Where'd you get that?" Lottie asked. The screen seemed to register this jealous question more than Boogie's recitation.

"High school. You remember those plays."

"That was, like, eight, ten years ago."

"Yeah, well, you know, it's poetry, so...." Boogie looked around, away.

"No, I don't know. No one remembers a thing like that unless he tries to."

Boogie kept looking away.

"Just what are you up to, my friend?"

"Nothin', man. Just...you know, whatever. We've all got our hobbies."

"Is that what you do while you're fishing, reciting poetry?"

Boogie's mouth held shut.

"You're not really fishing all that time, are you? What is this, then? You an actor? You wanna be an actor?"

Boogie trembled a little like he had when he'd first met the aliens. "The thought has crossed my mind."

The white screen began to register their emotions in denser patterns of lines and shapes but with nothing resembling written words of the human variety.

Boogie did not turn to look but saw the black lines projected onto Lottie's face. "Alright. I'm taking a few acting classes. So what?"

"Nothing," Lottie said, relaxing his pose. "No, that's just...why didn't you say anything before?"

"You know how it is, with the guys 'n' whatever. Word gets out...you know."

"Yeah." Lottie turned and stared at the screen. "No, man, that's your problem. You keep it all locked away, saved up. You live in that trailer like you're saving for a house, you never actually tell Andie how you feel, not that it would do you any good, and you don't tell even me or Carly that you want to act. Who knows, man? Lookin' at you, you could be, like, the next Michael McConaughey or somethin.'"

"Matthew."

"What?"

"Nothing. Never mind," Boogie said.

"Look at you. You don't think you can, so you take half measures. Think about it, though. Who else is ripping it up when we're out? You remember those days at Scully's, you could stand on top of your chair, beer in your hand, and start tearin' into everyone there, and they loved you for it."

"Not everyone."

Lottie looked at him, hands on his hips. "No, and I'll be blunt now. Don't cast your pearls before swine."

"She ain't swine."

"She's used up, man. Has been since the tenth grade. The world ran over her early, got what it wanted, and moved on. You should, too. There's no fixing that. Trust me, I've seen it before. You're not going to be her hero."

"Maybe if she sees my name up in lights."

"She's seen you all the time, in the flesh, for twenty years. You're too good for her, and she knows it."

Boogie, who had never thought himself above anyone, watched the screen write what he was feeling in a language he could not understand. "I've got a good job. I wouldn't want to lose that."

"Yeah, alright. I get it. But, like you like to say, you're 'livin' free.' Nothing's tying you down. Nothing but a misplaced devotion."

"She's a good person."

Lottie sighed. "Maybe she is, somewhere deep down. Maybe there is a pearl trapped in that colorful shell. I don't know, Boogie. I just see it different. Carly, too."

Boogie pressed his fingertips against the white wall. It was warm but not hot. It tingled with a little electricity, which hummed along his palms when he pressed them in.

"Where are these classes, anyway? Where do you find something like that around here?" Lottie asked.

Without turning, Boogie said, "Mostly online. In-person stuff a couple nights a month in Fort Worth."

"And what do they say, the teachers?"

Boogie nodded, turned, and let a smile escape. "You know, like I've got something. It's going somewhere." He breathed in and out heavily. "Whoo. Alright. Now that we have fully emoted, how do we get out of here?"

Lottie walked past him and tried the door again, but no amount of fiddling with the handle or pulling on the door would make it budge. "Maybe little Dorian is asleep."

"Or on the shitter, though I'm not sure those little bodies do much digesting. What do you think they eat?"

"Besides people? I don't know. Salamanders, maybe." More loudly, Lottie said, "Y'all eat salamanders? Mark it on the board. One for yes, two for no."

An X shape appeared very strongly on the screen.

"One X. You got it, Lottie. They eat salamanders. I bet they eat other amphibians, too."

"No, hold on now. That X has two lines in it. So maybe that's a no." To the screen, Lottie said, "Show me your word for yes."

At that, the little gray alien opened the flimsy wooden door and walked through.

"Alright," Lottie said. "Good to see you, Dorian. We've been waitin' here quite a while. You done with us for today?

Can I get home and eat now? Me hungry." He rubbed circles around his belly.

The gray alien the men called Dorian extended its right arm, gesturing for them to walk through the door into the office beyond. Lottie led, and Boogie followed.

As Boogie passed Dorian, who did not move or turn its head, he sensed something inside the alien's large, bulbous head. It was another presence that somehow turned and followed him as he walked past. As he studied this presence, he felt it reciprocate his attention with great, angry heat. Boogie's eyelids fluttered low, but he regained his composure and walked through the door, into the rest of the trailer.

4

The trailer was empty. None of the construction plans for the subdivision were laid out. They were not rolled up anywhere else.

"You see what I'm seeing, Boogie?"

"Yep."

"This is some kind of replica."

"Maybe."

"It's a bit too neat in here."

Boogie studied the trailer, scanning the large, flat desks and empty walls. "There's no paper anywhere. No wall calendar, nothing."

Dorian walked past them and led them to the end of the trailer, where a pad of company stationery rested on one of the desks. A cup full of markers and pens sat ahead of it, under the blinded window. The small gray alien gestured for one of the men to sit down and write.

"I went first with the massage," Boogie said.

Lottie shot out some breath. "Sure. It's just a little writing, right?" He smiled toward Dorian, saying, "I'll check the chair for probes, of course." He sat down and shook his arms loose.

Boogie looked back around the rest of the trailer. "I don't see that white screen in here."

"Whatever," Lottie said. "Let's just get this over with. I'm starving, too." He picked up a ballpoint pen and wrote:

Dear Carly, Becca and Allie–
Things have gotten a little strange lately. I think I am of sound mind and body, but me and Boogie have been having some kind of experiences we can't explain.

He looked at Dorian, who evinced no response, and continued writing:

Anyway, believe it or not, it's like we've been abducted by aliens, kinda sorta, but they just seem to be testing us out. I don't know why. One is standing next to me right now. Boogie named him Dorian. He doesn't ever say anything and I think he might be a puppet or something.

Boogie saw dark shadows splashing on the paper.

"Right," Lottie said. "Here we go. The paper is the white screen now."

"Naw, I think it's storming outside. You can see it through the blinds. Here." Boogie reached across the desk to peek through the blinds and saw white light. The ground was a swirl of dark, like black ink being stirred into a bowl of milk. A wave of intense, angry heat washed over him. "I guess not."

"Guess I better finish, then," Lottie said and returned to his letter.

As it stands, your Uncle Boogie just tried to open the blinds in the office, but Dorian got angry. This happens from time to time when we exceed our boundaries. We have to go through all their hoops before we're let go.

Lottie raised his head in thought. "Now what?" he asked, but not to Boogie or Dorian specifically.

"I dunno," Boogie said. "Tell them what we've been doing. Make a record of it."

So, Lottie wrote:

The first thing we did was play poker with the aliens. Taught them how. A white screen recorded our activity. Then our bodies were scanned through our feet.

Lottie smiled at his word choice. "That's a nice way to put it," he said before he continued writing.

Those were two different times. Just now we were led into Lou's office, but it was empty, and we started acting like Shakespeare monkeys to entertain them. This worked, but now I am here, writing this letter, surrounded by three walls and unable to go free until these aliens are satisfied.

I love you all very much and miss you and when I'm done being held captive...

Dark clouds passed over the paper as Lottie grew sad.

However this letter gets to you, be safe and pray to Jesus. All this does cause me to think and reflect. It might be better...

He paused and looked at Dorian. "No one's gotta see this, right?" he asked.

"Doesn't seem that way to me," Boogie replied.

Lottie scratched out "be better" and wrote:

It might be who of us—

"Behoove," Boogie corrected.

Lottie looked up at him angrily.

"Sorry."

Lottie curled his arm around the paper and scratched out "be who of us."

It might behoove us to get married.
Love,
Lottie (your Dad)

Lottie handed the letter to Dorian, who made no gesture to accept it. Lottie stood up and tried to hand it to Dorian again. Finally, he folded the paper neatly and tucked it into his shirt pocket.

Dorian gestured for Boogie to sit.

"Your turn, I guess," Lottie said.

"My turn," echoed Boogie, sitting down. Boogie stared at the paper for a while, twirling the pen in his hand.

"Everything all right?" Lottie asked.

"Yeah, just thinking," he answered. After a minute of staring at the blank paper, Boogie noticed a few dark lines slip through the window blinds. "I don't know what to do."

Lottie noticed the activity on the blinds increase.

"I ain't got no one, Lottie, except you." The shadows fell more frequently. "And you've got Carly and the kids, and you're always with them, rightfully so." The room was darkening with the density of the sharpening shadows. "All I got is work and fishing and acting and that dumb drunken slut Andie I chase around and for no good reason like a goddamned fool."

"Hey, man," Lottie said, massaging Boogie's shoulders. "Don't put yourself down. She ain't really like that. She just plays because that's all she knows how. Look, why don't you write Andie a letter? Tell her how you feel. She'll never have to see it."

"Alright, but don't you go readin' it neither." Boogie began:

Dear Andie:

It's Boogie, your friend, J.B. We've known each other since grade school and I've always had my eye on you. But you know that. You lead me around like a fool.

The black lines from the blinds began to take on more determined shapes on the paper as Boogie continued.

No, that's not what I want to say. I love you. You are smarter than you think you are. You're smarter than all of us combined. But you hang around with drunken rednecks because no one ever told you better. When I see you with others during the day, I see how smart and sweet you are. I sometimes come around the yard of the old folks' home just to watch you smile with people and make them feel good. But I work, too, and can usually only catch you at night, when you forget all that. You always play up or down to those around you.

The blinds began rattling, as if a breeze had found its way through the window or a large truck was passing by. Lottie looked over at the gray alien, who was leaning against the wall. "Go on, Boogie, keep doing what you're doing."

Boogie continued:

You deserve better. I'm not saying that I deserve you, but I'll treat you like the woman I know you are. I'll make you want to smile. You know I've got a good job and I'm not a drunk. I want a nice family. I know your family didn't give you much to go on but mine did, and they're gone now, so let me teach you true love. I love you. I love you. I love you.

Love,

John "Boogie" Bouguereau

With that, Boogie set his elbows on the desk, held his head in his hands, and cried. He cried for several minutes, all while the blinds leaped into a frenzy and the shadows it let through swirled onto the page. Those shadows threatened to camouflage and cancel out all that Boogie had written.

As his eyes dried, he saw the shadows obscuring his words. He stood and looked angrily at the gray alien, who was slightly hunched over.

Lottie said, "Man, whatever you wrote, I think you started to break the system. Maybe they don't got categories for that."

Boogie quickly ripped the page from the pad, folded it hastily, and tucked it into his pants pocket, leaving it unzipped. "Come on, let's go," he said. He walked determinedly to the door of the trailer, opened it himself, and walked through. Lottie followed him into the bright late afternoon sky filled with a goldening sun.

Lou, their foreman, walked toward them. "You guys looking for your checks? Sorry 'bout that. Be right there."

Boogie and Lottie, befuddled, turned around and followed Lou back into the trailer. As he opened the door, an alligator lizard, about two feet long, sprang out. "Whoa!" Lou cried, jumping backward into Lottie. "You two goddamned jokers." He caught his breath. "What in the hell are you doin' to me?"

Lottie looked back at Boogie, who could already see through the door into the messy trailer. When they re-entered, all seemed as normal. The trailer was filled with blueprints and papers. The blinds were open. The doors to the offices at each end, where Dorian had taken them, were open. All was as per usual.

"You two alright?" Lou asked, handing them their checks.

"Yeah," Lottie said. "Long day, I guess. Come on, Boogie. Let's go eat, huh?"

"Yeah," Boogie said. "Scully's is just a mile down from here. First round's on me."

A few minutes later, at Scully's, Boogie and Lottie sat with their beers, eyes drooping. "I always regret these nachos," Boogie said. "Why do I keep coming back to them?"

"I don't know, but I tell you what. I'm exhausted. Feels like I've been up all night."

"Tough week o' work. Your body's catching up already."

Lottie jumped in his seat and pulled out his phone. "Damn! Boogie, what the hell am I doing here? I gotta be home with Carly. Damn! Sorry, man. You know what? Come on over. Carly 'n' the kids'll wanna see you. Why are we even at this dive?"

The two men stood up while Boogie reached in his pants pocket to pay. A piece of paper fell out, but Boogie was too tired to pick it up.

"What're you doing?" Lottie asked.

"I told you I'd get the rounds at Scully's."

"When'd you say that?"

"I'm sure I did. Don't worry about it."

"What's with those pants, anyway? Zippers?"

"They're waterproof. With these tucked into my boots, I stay dry on the excavator. Nothing worse than sitting on a soggy ass."

"You wear those out to party, that's why you ain't got no girlfriend."

"There's my Boogie Woogie," came a voice dancing from across the room.

"Hey, Andie," Boogie said.

"Come on, whatcha doin'? Show me your moves."

"Hey, look, I'm kinda tired right now. Gonna head out."

She put on a pouty face and said, "And leave me alone with all these fools?"

"Look, I'm just not—"

"What's this?" she asked, picking up the folded-up piece of paper that had fallen out of his pocket.

"I dunno. A packing receipt or something."

"Dear Andie," she read. "Oooh, a letter for me?" she said, flashing her eyelashes.

"Yep. Must be," Boogie replied. "You know what she's up to?" he asked Lottie. "You see what I gotta deal with?"

"You love it, man."

Boogie put on a slight smile and turned back to Andie, who looked up at him with frightened, serious eyes.

"What're you doing?" he asked. He reached for the paper, but she pulled it away and walked toward the door slowly, reading the letter. She turned to him then bolted out the door toward her car.

"What the hell?"

"What, you write her a love letter?"

"No, man, it's a goddamn packing slip. She's high or something."

"You better go after her!" Lottie said. "Now's your chance, Boogieman."

"Chance for what?" Boogie said.

Lottie stared at him, as did one or two other men in the bar.

One of them, an old acquaintance named Petey Penhollow, shrugged his shoulders in wonderment at Boogie. He said, "She pulls up a letter that starts 'Dear Andie' and runs away, Boogie? You'd better go make up her mind for her, whatever it's about."

Lottie kicked him in the pants.

Boogie got in his truck, having seen the direction Andie

had taken. "Dear Andie...Dear Andie. Boogie, what have you done? What dumbass thing have you been doing without remembering?" He caught up to her slowly, not wanting to frighten her. He followed from a little distance down empty country roads. The clouds had parted to reveal a field of stars. Boogie pulled into her driveway just as she was closing her front door. He ran up and knocked, but she didn't answer. He knocked again then, after a moment, turned the handle and walked through. Andie lay on her couch, face down, the letter in her right hand.

"Andie, Andie, what's going on? You all right?"

"Go away," she replied, her voice muffled by the cushions. He pulled the letter from her hands, prying her fingers apart to do so. He read the letter.

Dear Andie, Boogie read. This was his handwriting. This was company stationery. He had gone into the trailer only to get his check this afternoon. Lunch had been under a tree, where he and the guys had been listing war movies, and when someone had mentioned *Crimson Tide*, Boogie had compared it to *Run Silent, Run Deep*, which had been met with silence and deep stares. That was not what he faced in the present moment, when Andie had really been moved by something he had written but could not remember. Boogie drank, but he had never blacked out. He could have written this letter—these were his feelings but feelings expressed as if he were seventeen again, watching her drive off from a party with another guy. Boogie would do what the guys at Scully's had told him to do—he would make up her mind for her.

"Look, uh, I'm sorry if any of this hurt you. I suppose I just needed, at some point, to express my own feelings. I'm not sure I meant for you to see this." She lay there, silently, her chest heaving sharply. Boogie massaged her shoulder. "You crying? Andie, turn around."

She did, revealing bloodshot eyes. "I can't," she said.

"Can't what?"

"I don't know how."

"Don't know how to what?"

"To love you back. I've got nothing."

"Well here, give me your hand," he said, taking both of her hands in his. "Now you've got something." He pulled her up, and she didn't resist. He held her in his arms for a while, and the two sat silently. "Here," he said, and he lay down on the couch, pulling her in alongside him. After a brief moment, she got up and began taking off his shoes. "What are you doin'?" he asked.

"No shoes on my couch." When she finished and had tossed them off to the side, she looked at him and said, "There. All better."

Boogie looked at Andie, sitting over him. This was everything he had ever wanted, even more than sex. She fidgeted with her hands in her lap and looked away.

There. All better. Those words brought an image to his mind. He remembered that blurry picture from his phone of him lying on a bed with his shoes off. It was more than a recollection of looking through his camera roll with Lottie last week. He had been there.

Boogie sat up. "Something's wrong, Andie."

"I'll say. Now you're the one looking at me funny."

"That letter. I don't recall ever writing it. And now I'm remembering other things I don't remember."

Andie stood up. "Just relax, J.B. I'll go fetch us some beers from the fridge."

She took longer to do this than Boogie thought she should. He heard her thumbs tapping a text into her phone. He lay down to try to bring the passing image back, to grab hold of it as a memory. Very soon, he fell asleep.

5

About six weeks later, Boogie accompanied Lottie, Carly, and their kids to a fair on the grounds of the high school. Lottie, for reasons he told Boogie he could not fully explain, had felt compelled to visit Carly's father on his deathbed and ask his daughter's hand in marriage. This had pleased the sick old man, who'd died soon after. Knowing that her fiancé had done this had pleased Carly in ways she did not expect and also gave her the peace of knowing that her father had died happy. Aglow with the intensity of love and bittersweet grief, the two tried to console Boogie by making him share in their happiness. Andie had not called him back after the night Boogie had fallen asleep on her couch and had not shown up at Scully's again.

Boogie tried to play along in Meadrow family happiness by carrying their daughter Allie on his shoulders.

"Don't you worry about her," Carly said, taking Boogie's arm, which still grasped the girl's ankle. "You did the good thing. She's right, you know, it wouldn't work out. She needs someone not as good as you."

"That don't make no sense," Boogie said. "She needs a good man."

"You and her, you, like, speak different languages," Carly said. "You're like from different planets. She wouldn't know what to do with you nor you with her. Honestly, J.B., you're also maybe just a bit taken in by her beauty, which isn't gonna last much longer, trust me, and is already fading. You're maybe still stuck on the way you saw her in school is all."

"Yeah," was all Boogie could manage. He knew what she and Lottie had been saying was true. He knew it in his mind but not his heart. He looked around and saw a whack-a-mole. "Maybe that's just what I need." He cast his eyes upward at the little girl on his shoulders. "What do you say, Allie-gator?"

A little while later, growing tired of the sights, sounds, and smiles all around him, Boogie ducked into a funhouse. He looked at himself as he passed a row of distorting mirrors and entered a room whose floor spun him outward against the wall. He played against this, calculating how he could reach the light blue door across the room. Once through the door, he walked down a corridor that twisted until a wall became the floor and the floor a wall. "This is my life," he said. "Nothing what I want it to be, everything designed to chuck me out." At the end of the corridor, he found another light blue door. Before he opened it, he noticed that it had grown eerily silent, almost perfectly so. He walked through it.

He found himself in a room covered in mirrors. A chandelier in the center reflected dozens of bulbs into a galactic array against the shining facets on the walls, which seemed, to Boogie, to be undulating. Somehow, the mirrors, shaped as tall, thin diamonds, were flexing against each other on nearly invisible seams.

Boogie marveled at this for a while, reveling in his starry, cosmic solitude. He looked for his reflection, for his image floating somewhere in this candlelit, celestial sea. He could not find it. The blue door through which he had walked had disappeared. It was behind one of these mirrors. He laughed a little at the gag and walked around on the shining black stone that made up the floor of the room, which was about twelve feet square and just as high.

No matter where he went, the mirrors always turned away from him, hiding his reflection from him. He could see his own hands and feet as they reached away from him, but they did not appear on the folding wall of mirrors before him. He began to panic, as if he were being annihilated, his soul erased. "Alright now," he said and looked for the exit. He could not find it.

"Hello?" he called out and banged on the glass.

A wave of searing heat washed over him, and, in a moment, he remembered where he was. "This again. How long's it been now? Thought I was done with this. Lottie's not here, though. Lottie, you here?"

The mirrors folded in on themselves, shrinking the room to half its dimensions, six feet by six feet, just wide enough for the man to stretch out. The chandelier still hung well above him.

The mirrors undulated more fluidly now, and from within the many strange new reflections, Boogie's own began to emerge in multiple. He saw not one of himself but many, dozens all around him. They looked like him or were at least dressed like him, but the mirrors subtly distorted his face and body, making him look either sincere or devious, stiff or relaxed, welcoming or threatening. The bulbs of the chandelier sent out their rays through its many branches, and bouncing back and forth on each other, this produced a dark web over Boogie and all his reflections. He reached out, and many reflected hands reached back, all jostling to be the one to touch him. He felt a strange power in this, a control over these many versions of himself.

He looked up at the chandelier and back down again and was startled. He thought he saw a yellow-eyed dragon lurking within the reflections, slinking between the many versions of himself. "Dorian?" he called out timidly. "You there, little buddy?"

No one answered.

He held still, but the shadows changed all around him. The smooth, subtle distortions of the mirrors sent him off balance, and he closed his eyes just to keep upright. Even with his eyes closed, or perhaps all the more with them closed, he felt the other presence lurking around him. This was the presence he had felt watching him from inside Dorian's bulbous skull.

The presence evaded him, though. If he opened his eyes again, it fell away with the shadows racing toward the edge of his vision. If he turned his head, he grew dizzy, and the presence somehow mesmerized him for a moment.

Whatever this thing was, it wanted to hypnotize him and wrap around him like a snake. The mirrors themselves began to feel like its scales, slowly curling in on him, writhing as they tightened their grip.

He pounded on the mirrors again and felt wave after wave of searing heat. They were drawing closer, so close now that he could press his feet against them, one forward, one backward, to scramble upward toward the chandelier. This was the only unchanging object, his fixed point of reference, and the only way out. He endured the heat but slipped back onto the floor. He tried again a second time and slipped, not getting much higher. The third time he tried, he felt no heat. The walls had folded in more closely and grew more angled, providing sturdier stepping stones. He had nearly reached the chandelier, twelve feet above the floor, when, all at once, the walls flew back to their original dimensions, leaving Boogie in free fall.

He fell past where the floor should have been, into blackness. As he did, he saw Lottie entering the room and looking around. He continued to fall and saw Lottie looking downward, toward him, puzzled. Then the darkness grew thicker, as if the floor were growing solid again. All was black.

Boogie came to, face down, on what felt like concrete. He had not noticed himself pass out or fall asleep, and he had certainly not felt himself hit the floor, but here he was, and maybe he had hit so hard he had gone unconscious. The room smelled like cleaning spray. He remembered the Build-a-Burger, which had smelled the same way. He remembered the massage and every other experience with the aliens. He could be trapped in one of their rooms once again. He stood up and hit his head on something waist-high.

"Hello?" he called out. His voice did not echo. "Hello? Is there anybody there? Dorian? Lottie?"

Boogie rubbed his face vigorously. He did not know if he should dare walk around. He shuffled his feet forward and felt the concrete beneath him. With the smell of cleaning spray came a whiff of dirty mops. "Well, there's something normal, at least."

Suddenly, a blast of light shot into the space. The silhouette of a tall, slim figure appeared in the rectangle of white light. Boogie jerked back and fell against a row of mop handles.

"Boogie! There you are," came Lottie's voice. "What are you doing in the janitor's closet?"

"What? What?" Boogie called back, visibly shaking. He did not recognize the slop sink next to him. The room was about four feet square.

Lottie flipped the light switch, and Boogie saw everything more clearly. "We've been looking for you everywhere, man. Why are you hiding out in here? You're trembling. What's wrong?" Lottie stepped forward, letting the metal door behind him slam shut.

"I..." Boogie began. "The funhouse. That's where I was. God, it's good to see you." He began crying again. "I was in the funhouse, in the mirrors. Then it dropped me here. The dragon."

"The dragon? What are you talking about?"

"The monster, Lottie. The one we've been dealing with all this time. The one who was measuring us up all that time, playing poker and getting massaged."

"Alright now, Boogie. Alright. You're stressed out. Let's just get out of here. Here. Splash a little water on your face."

Boogie turned on the tap of the slop sink to wash his face while Lottie tried to open the door. It would not open.

"Eh, Houston, we've got a problem here," Lottie said.

Boogie tried to turn off the sink, but the tap would not close. "Lottie, man, I can't get this thing off."

"And I can't get this door open, neither."

"I'm telling you, they've got us again."

"Who?"

"The aliens, Lottie."

"Man, you hit your head or something. Just help me get this door open, and we'll get someone about the sink."

Boogie, though, knelt down below the sink to turn off the supply valve. It broke off in his hand.

"Now you've done it, Boogie. Come on. Let's knock this door down."

The two men rammed their shoulder against the door a few times. It did not budge. They banged on it loudly for several minutes to no response. Only once they stopped did they notice that the slop sink had filled and was spilling over.

"Now, what?" Lottie asked. "Alright. Well, someone'll notice this spilling out into the hallway of the school. Meanwhile, our shoes and socks are getting soaked."

"Is it just me," Boogie said, "or is the water level rising on the floor?"

"It shouldn't be. There's an undercut on the door, and it's got a vent on it. We're not going to drown in here."

The two men resumed banging on the metal door. After a few minutes of this, the water was knee deep.

"Time to call someone," Lottie said.

"Good idea," Boogie said. He took his phone out of his thigh pocket. "No signal."

"Me neither," Lottie said. "Uh...."

"Yeah," Boogie agreed.

"Maybe we can bang the door handle off with something."

"The only thing here is the spout itself. Maybe we can use it as a lever."

Lottie pondered the prudence of this while watching Boogie unscrew the spout from the sink. The water gushed upward. The spout had no mass to bear against the door handle and broke in half when used as a lever.

"Back to square one," Lottie said and immediately shot his head upward in recognition. "That's right. That's what this is, Boogie. Square one. Them aliens."

"That's what I've been trying to say."

The water was chest deep now.

"What kind of test is this?" Lottie asked. "Let's try our phones again."

"No signal, Lottie. I think the aliens have jammed us."

Neither man spoke, as the water rose to their chins.

They looked up at the hatch in the low ceiling above.

"An HVAC hatch?" Lottie asked. "Big enough for both of us." He reached up and pushed against the hatch, which gave freely. He smiled at Boogie, who immediately jumped upward. His side of the hatch gave way. But it was hinged in the middle. Only one body would fit through at a time.

The water filled the closet nearly to the ceiling, and both men would soon drown. Boogie knew they would find something dangerous above them, some final test. The light from the incandescent bulb, unaffected by the water, cast a greenish glow on their faces. Once they were fully underwater, Lottie gestured to Boogie that he would go up first.

Boogie shook his head. The light flickered. He pointed

to Lottie and counted on his fingers to four then pinched Lottie's ring finger. He pointed to himself and held up one index finger.

Lottie nodded in agreement.

Boogie pulled himself upward, through his side of the hatch, and sat on the edge. He could still see Lottie below. All was black above. As he had calculated, the displacement left new air for Lottie to breathe. "You alright down there?" he called.

"Yeah."

"The water still flowing?"

Lottie put his hand over the open faucet. "No."

"Figured." Boogie looked around at the space above him. All was black. He could make out nothing. Even the light coming up from the janitor's closet hit nothing. He looked down at Lottie again. "I'll help you up if you want, but maybe it's better if you stick with Carly and the kids, you know?"

"I ain't—" Lottie started to say when the water rushed out of the room and took Lottie with it.

Boogie pulled his legs up to lie down and intended to poke his head back through the hatch to see who had opened the door below, but the hatch had closed tight, and he could not get it open again. As he lay there on his belly, he knocked on the hatch. No one knocked back. He was on his own. He had to slay this dragon alone.

"That's alright," Boogie said. "I know how this ends. Boogie wins with a flush."

6

Boogie stood up. Wherever he was—on a ship, in another dimension—this part of it was in total darkness. He ran his hands through his wet hair a few times to keep water from dripping down his face. The splatter of the drops wrung from his hair hitting the floor was the only sound that accompanied his heavy breathing and the buzz of his central nervous system.

"I'm here, Dorian," Boogie said.

After a few seconds of silence, he heard something like switches flicking on. Six walls lit up in a dull gray color. The room was hexagonal, the same room in which he and Lottie had met the first trio of gray aliens. He walked around the room. A puddle of water marked where he had originally stood. The gray walls recorded nothing. He walked up to the one of them and pressed his hand against it. Nothing happened.

He turned around and jumped, startled at the sight of Andie, who stood where his puddle of water had been. "Andie," he said and walked toward her, but some primitive part of his brain seized his muscles. He studied her for a while and relaxed. He looked around the room. "Nice try," he said. "That ain't her."

No response came.

"Alright, maybe this is your test. You want me to tell you why I know this isn't her? Okay...." He walked forward to study the specimen. "I don't know why I should be helping you replicate human beings. But if it gets me out of here...." The replica stood still and calm, a slight smile on its face. "Same height, same build...." He drew closer, looking it up and down. "Maybe you even got her DNA somehow, off a beer glass or something. Maybe that's what you did to the girl from the Build-A-Burger."

Boogie came all the way around and stood before the model. "You talk?"

"Hey, Boogie," came the voice, soft but accurate. It was the way he had often wanted to hear Andie's voice, calm and soothing.

"Alright...." He tapped his chin. "But what are we missing here? A soul? That's for sure. Maybe it's as simple as that. But maybe you get this thing out on the dance floor, surrounded by a bunch of guys wearing beer goggles, and they won't know the difference. Come on now, Andrea McAllister, show me your moves."

Music came on loudly in the hexagonal room, and the humanoid Andie began dancing. It was awkward and clumsy at first, but as the machine continued, its movements grew smoother and more subtle. Its slender fingertips reached toward the ceiling, twisting and turning with the rest of the body below. A smile grew on its face, one that Boogie matched.

He clapped his hands twice, and the music stopped. The machine stopped dancing and stood still again, hands at its sides, still smiling.

"That's where it is," Boogie said. "That's where your problem lies. Right there, in that smile. Find out moonshine, Andie. Find out moonshine."

The replicant tried on many subtle variations of the smile while Boogie watched.

"No, nope. Not it. Not gonna get it. You do not understand. You cannot replicate her true beauty. You cannot replicate her pain. That's what it is, you see. That's her secret. She's locked in a tower, and every guy, me included, wants to be the one to slay the dragon and get to her. But she don't want to be got. She made the tower. The pain is real, and so is the smile. With her, you don't get one without the other. You figure a way to make a robot feel pain and yet to want to live, well, then you'll be more convincing."

The replicant hunched its shoulders, and its jaw fell slack. This look, which he had seen on the massage girl, terrified him. It was the death of a thing not yet living. He breathed sharp breaths, and the replica fell to the floor in a pile.

A few seconds later, the gray walls turned white and filled with writing. The writing grew denser and denser until most of the light left the room. Boogie turned around to look at the wall behind him then turned back again. He heard another switch, and the room went first completely dark and then, a second later, bright again. Nothing was on the walls.

A replica of Lottie stood before him.

"Alright, here we go," Boogie said. "Much better this time."

"Oh, God, Boogie, that is you!" the imitation Lottie said. "Hell, man. After you climbed up here, I got flushed out of the room. They had some kind of electromagnetic lock on the door is what I'm guessing. Water everywhere. I was just standing up again when they beamed me up here. You alright?"

Boogie, warily, replied, "Yeah, Lottie. I'm doin' alright. We gotta figure this one out before we can get you back to Carly and the kids."

"Okay, okay," fake Lottie replied. "What do we do?"

"We gotta figure out how you're a fake."

"Fake?" the machine asked, pulling its head back. "What do you mean, me a fake?"

"What I mean is, they just had a fake Andie up here, standing right where you are. I figured out how she was a phony, a cheap imitation. Now it's your turn. See, the way I figure, they only ever got to here through my thoughts or something. But they've got you felt through, from all our experiences. So, let's have it."

"Have what, Boogie? It's me, man. Feel. Take my hand."

Boogie shook its hand and felt the firm, familiar grip of his friend. He grabbed the wrist and pulled it up to his face, looking for fingerprints, which were there. The hands were worn with work. "Huh, maybe it is you, after all. Alright, then. Sorry about that. Let's see how we get out of here."

The two men looked around the room.

"You here, Dorian?" Lottie asked.

"I think he's out of the picture now. I think we did him

in back in the trailer." A thought sprang into Boogie mind, and he resisted showing it. "You got your phone? Maybe we can just call. Maybe it's as simple as that."

Lottie patted his pants. "No, you know. Left it in the truck, like usual."

"Nuh uh," Boogie said.

"What do you mean, 'nuh uh'? You know me."

"You just used it to call for help. We had no signal, remember?"

"Well, I don't know," fake Lottie said. "Maybe it got lost in the shuffle. The flush, as it were. Why don't you call?"

"Because my phone has recently been submerged in water."

"Right." The humanoid Lottie looked, at that moment, the most human it ever had, for Boogie could see in that expression the realization that this should have been its first excuse for not using the phone.

Despite him catching this Lottie as a fake, it did not drop its jaw and fall like fake Andie had or like the massage girl had when Lottie had said something about her having a pimp. This gave Boogie an idea. He had to make the hidden dragon angry.

Boogie squared up to fake Lottie. "Carly would never let you leave without the phone, anyway."

"That is correct," fake Lottie said. "She's always on me about that."

"Nuh uh," Boogie said. "You act like she's on your case about certain things, but you're the one who would never leave that phone behind. Why not just admit you love your wife and kids?"

Fake Lottie said, "Of course I love my wife and kids."

"No, come on, say it with real meaning. Let me give you some acting training. Really dig in, Lottie. Go to that place where your deepest love lives."

"I love my wife and kids," fake Lottie said, with a tremble in its voice.

"Again," Boogie said.

"I love my wife and kids," the replica said, with a slight metallic creak in its voice.

"Again. Really dig deep."

"I love them." The voice was going deeper and starting to distort.

"We're almost there. Really dig deep now, down to the deepest hell you'd go to to rescue them."

The replicant dropped its head, looking at Boogie with increasingly menacing eyes. "I love my wife and kids."

"Yeah, tell me how you love them."

The eyes began searing and the fingers stiffening.

"You love that woman."

Something held the machine back. Some force operating through the machine wanted to harm Boogie, and some greater force held it back.

He pressed on. "You love and obey that good woman. You love her, and you give your whole life to her."

A coolness washed over the machine. Its shoulders drooped.

"Gotcha." He walked up to the dead machine and poked one of its shoulders. It fell to the ground in a pile.

In an instant, all of the walls turned off, leaving the room in total darkness. When they came on again, dimly,

Boogie found himself staring across the room at an exact copy of himself, wet clothes and all.

"Well now," the replica said. "This must be the final test."

Boogie looked around the hexagonal room for some point of reference, where he knew his own body had been in reference to fake Andie and fake Lottie. All he saw were wet footprints everywhere.

He made himself sensitive to the expansion and contraction of his own chest. He felt his own body from within, the coursing of his blood and vibration of his nerves. He was certain that he was not the copy.

Boogie said, "Alright, then, let's take the test. Let's get acquainted. My name is John Bouguereau, called Boogie by my closest friends and dearest enemies. What's your name?"

The other Boogie said, "That's my name, but you would know what Andie and Carly call me because they think Boogie is a stupid nickname."

Boogie, recognizing that fake Boogie would test him to prove he was the real one, realized he had to come up with an honest answer. "J.B."

"Alright, alright," the other Boogie said. "Naturally, this is how the scene would play out. Next, I suppose, we should compare scars. That sound fair?"

Boogie nodded, but his knees locked at the prospect of coming too near a perfect copy of himself. The other Boogie did not have this hangup and walked over. It rolled up its right sleeve to reveal a gash made not long ago by a wire cable that snapped as he pulleyed his boat back onto its trailer. Boogie showed the same scar.

"One for one," Boogie said. His voice quivered. "Good

job. Now let's see the birthmark in the shape of Cuba on the upper left arm."

"I don't have one of those," the copy said.

"Neither do I. But you have memories, right?"

"Course I do. They're all *my* memories. You go ahead and recall them. It just means that you recorded my brain while I was asleep just now."

"You remember all the different episodes of this little adventure? The name of our little gray friend?"

"Dorian, of course. But I'm the one who should be testing you. Tell me: when I was watching the house burn down, and Mom and Dad were in the ambulance losing their lives, what was the sound I fixated on?"

Boogie paused a moment. The aliens really had made a perfect copy of him. He had not recalled this particular memory in many years. "A blue jay."

Both bodies hung still, each beginning to doubt its own originality.

"Well, what do you say?" Boogie asked. "How do we get out of here?"

"You tell me."

"Way I figure, we've got to prove to the dragon somehow which one of us is the real John Bouguereau and which is the fake. Hell, maybe it did such a great job that even it doesn't know anymore. Maybe the fake one of us doesn't even know it's fake."

"Seems natural," the other Boogie replied. "But you've got to ask a more essential question first. That is, why create a copy? To infiltrate society? What society have I got? Tri-County Excavation?"

At watching his copy feel sorry for itself, a thing the real Boogie did all too easily, an idea came into his mind.

Boogie stood and walked to the center of the hexagonal room. "Let me ask you a question: Why did you fall asleep right away on Andie's couch that night? You could've kept on trying."

"I was just tired, exhausted from all this. You forget how much your emotions exhaust you. You didn't remember going through all this, but your body did. Then you've got Andie within reach, finally, and then your doubts about remembering things, and it all hits you at once."

"My emotions really are exhausting, aren't they?" Boogie said. "You guys use them to record us. These white walls, black lines, no color. You don't get how our emotions work, but you can use them. You can't feel them, so they drain you down, too. That's how poor little Dorian got done in. All that love I showed for Andie in the letter. No, it wasn't my love for Andie that did little Dorian in, was it?"

The other Boogie cocked its head. "Then, what would you say it was?"

"My love for me," Boogie said. "Isn't that all that courage is, enough self-love to stay alive?"

The other Boogie put its hands on its hips.

"And with enough courage, a man will die for others. He'll love himself into them, forever."

"Where're you going with this?" the other Boogie said.

"I'm saying you guys are going to have to go through me to get to anyone else."

The other Boogie stared at him, without anger or fear, with none of the draconian hate he had seen in the other fakes. Boogie felt his heart beat and his breath enter and leaves his lungs. He was at a stalemate with the other.

"I know who I am," Boogie said.

"And what makes you think I don't?" the other Boogie said.

"Because I made all those wet footprints before. They all led to me. As a wise man once said, 'Boogie wins with a flush.'"

The other Boogie knit its brow, scanned the floor, which had mostly dried, spread its arms a little in exasperation, and let them fall again. "If you say so."

Then, all went black.

Boogie found himself, a second later, standing behind the school cafeteria. He saw some dogs tear apart the garbage, in which there was what looked like a pair of whole, uncooked turkeys.

"Boogie, hey," Lottie said, embracing him. "You made it out of there."

Boogie looked at his old friend, the real Lottie. "Yeah. Barely. You remember all that now?"

"Yeah. I don't think those memories are going away any time soon."

"You're still dripping wet," Boogie said.

"It's only been a few minutes. I was just looking for a way onto the roof to find you when I caught you here. So, what happened up there?"

Boogie told him the story.

"I don't get it," Lottie said. "How do you know that the footprints weren't the other guy's?"

Boogie turned and nodded toward the dogs tearing

apart the turkeys. "That part doesn't matter, I think. None of those questions mattered. We were in a stalemate."

"What makes the difference, then? How'd you win?"

"I'm not sure I've won, not just yet," Boogie said.

"What, uh, what do you mean?" Lottie said.

Boogie looked at Lottie. His friend had taken one step back and had his hands on his hips, not resting on them, but one near the phone in his back pocket, both ready to throw. Boogie was going to have to prove to his friend he was the real John Bouguereau.

He turned back to face the dogs tearing apart the turkeys. "When I was a kid, a cousin used to come over and play. Kind of a weird fellow, but whatever. He finds a mouse one day and ties its leg to a string and that string to a heavy stick. Then he brings the whole kit over to our cat, there on the back deck. The cat just stares at the mouse for a while, totally uninterested. Then my cousin says, 'Watch this,' and he cuts the string. The mouse starts running. The cat goes wild and grabs it."

"Your point being...?"

"My point being, I'm the mouse cut loose."

"You just going to wait for them to grab you?" Lottie said.

Boogie squatted down. In the darkness, the dogs' white teeth stood out the most. "No. Nor am I going to run like a mouse. It's time for me to live my own life."

Lottie said, "You don't suppose those are the leftover grays, do you? The ones they made into Andie and me?"

Boogie stood up. "Maybe. If so, where's the third one, for fake Boogie?"

Lottie looked back at him, cautiously.

"Maybe they'll keep trying," Boogie said. "I'll just have to keep a step ahead of them. Show the world the real me."

7

About three and a half years later, Boogie, after moving to California, found himself in Texas again, though in some part of the Prairies and Lakes he did not know well. He drove to the end of a road, where the GPS voice told him to turn right. He looked up to the crescent moon, the only thing populating a bare blue sky, and back down at his gauges. Ten thousand cicadas, hiding somewhere in broad daylight, sang above the low rumble of his idling engine. He looked left, where the shade of thick trees cast patterns of black shadow on the red dirt road. After this moment's pause, he obeyed the GPS and turned right. He followed that road for about a quarter of a mile before arriving at his destination.

He pulled into the driveway of a small white house set back from the road, eyeing the children's play set on the lawn. He rang the doorbell but heard from behind him, "J.B.!" He turned to see Andie holding a young baby in her arms. "There you are!" she went on.

"Hey, Andie," Boogie replied, walking down the stoop to greet her. They embraced briefly but tightly. She was not as thin as he remembered.

"Thanks for coming," she said, biting her lower lip.

"And who's this?" he asked, playfully and politely.

"This is Grace," she replied. "Her big sister Ella is in town with her dad."

"George, right?"

"You know, yes," Andie replied with a little twist, a little dance with the baby.

"I popped in at your wedding, you know."

"I know. Lottie told me. How's he doing?"

"He's fine, just fine. Carly, too. Kids are growin'."

"What about you? Anyone special, one of those Hollywood girls?" she asked, flashing her eyelashes a little. She still had a bit of her spark, Boogie noticed.

"You know me, Andie."

She rocked baby Grace back and forth, seeming to search for a response. "Well, hey. Let me take you inside, show you around our little place. You thirsty?"

"Sure, what have you got?"

"Iced tea, soda, beer," she offered, as they walked into the house. Boogie noticed a bit of a musty carpet smell.

"Iced tea'd be great." He watched her navigate her kitchen, watched her trace the life she'd made. "Things seem good for you, Andie. Things came around for you."

She looked at him and handed him his glass then turned around to pour her own. When she turned around again and sat down at the small round table, she leaned forward and said, "Thanks to you."

"Thanks to me? I'd a given you a house and kids myself."

"I know, I know." She paused. "You made me believe in myself."

"So much so you run off?"

"It's what I needed, J.B. To get away from Scully's and Fox Corners and the whole thing." She paused, her shoulders hunched, then continued, "You can handle all that and stay the same. You were right in your letter. I played to an audience. Up for the old folks, down for the rednecks. Look, how do I say this? It's like the old folks were just like the guys at the bar. I was never really being myself. And you, I didn't know how to be with you. How to.... But you're so good."

"I'm not so good, Andie. What do I do that isn't for myself?" he replied.

"Hold on there, J.B. Look. Out here, with my cousins, I get some normalcy. A little up, a little down. George is like that. It's real, it isn't perfect, which is what I need."

Boogie sat there for a while, looking around at the cabinets, into the next room, out the window.

Andie continued, "I watched your movie, you know. You were really good."

"It was just a bit part."

"Yeah, but it's a good start. I was so proud, we all are. Our Boogie Woogie, movie star. But you could always do that, back in school, even at the bar. What's your secret?"

Boogie thought a moment. "You remember, I don't know, about fourth or fifth grade, that magician who came to school? He had us all on the carpet in the library."

Andie nodded searchingly.

"Yeah, you remember. What he did was he opened this book full of line drawings, of kids and things, and he would pretend to suck up the color of our clothes and reopen the book, and there they were, colored onto the page. You don't remember that?"

"Yeah, no, that's ringing a bell. I maybe remember it a little differently somehow."

"Well, anyway, what's important is this, I'd say: all that magician did was pick the kids whose clothes he could already find in the book. All he had to do to trick us was make us believe we were seeing something new. He was only filtering information to us from the vast array of data out there."

"Okay...."

Boogie continued, "You can make a whole figure out of just enough parts. You pick out what's important. People will fill in the rest. It's a thing machines can't do because they don't realize that what we people recognize in each other is some little bit of ourselves."

Andie searched his face for a clue. "Well, I suppose that's all the magic they teach you in acting school. I just hope it means I see you holding that golden Oscar man one day."

The conversation turned to pleasantries: where Andie was working (she wasn't), what George was doing for a living (auto mechanic), how they'd met (her cousins), and so on. They took a tour of the house on foot then a tour of the three acres by sight, which included her fledgling garden and George's ongoing project, an old Camaro on cinder blocks. The kids, she said, took up all her time, but she wouldn't trade them for the world. After an hour or so, Andie and Boogie said goodbye, promising to keep up.

"Alright, take care, Andie."

"You, too, J.B."

Boogie turned around in the driveway, driving over the

lawn a little, and headed out. A sadness welled up within him until he could feel it in his lower lip. With that sadness came another feeling, exuberance. The thing that he had once built up in his mind to be everything now fit into his rearview mirror.

After a short quarter mile, he found his way back to the intersection. The dark road ahead was a little brighter now, the sun finding its angle through the trees. He drove past the intersection, against the instructions of the GPS, through those trees. Golden sunlight and dim shadow formed a web that crawled across his truck as he drove. He felt those lines trace their way across his face, writing the signs and symbols of a secret language he was only now learning to speak, forming a man, all gold and shadows, for the world to behold.

ABOUT THE AUTHOR

Peter A. Heasley is a priest and professor of Scripture in New York City. His short fiction and poetry criticism have appeared in *Dappled Things*, the *Saturday Evening Post*, and *Presence*. *Kirkus Reviews* has acclaimed his novels as "measured and painterly...constructing a story that feels very much its own" (for *Under a Darkening Moon*).

His novels include:

Under a Darkening Moon
Within a Wakening Earth
Into a Hearkening Sky
The Shadow of Two Suns

www.ingramcontent.com/pod-product-compliance
Lightning Source LLC
Chambersburg PA
CBHW030946310726
48969CB00008B/2394